THE ADVENTURES OF A SKETCH DIARY

COLLEEN A. COFFMAN

Illustrated by
COLLEEN A. COFFMAN

Edited by
AMY L. COFFMAN MASSEY

HANGAR 1 PUBLISHING

This book is dedicated to my mom and dad (who started this whole thing, to begin with), to my siblings (who still love and support me, despite my weirdness), to my children and grandchildren (who love and/or tolerate the stories), my dear Philip (who held my hand through the lost and found years) and to my beloved Faeries (who are always in my heart and magically in my life).

CONTENTS

FIREFLIES

As a young child, I recall the hues:
Vibrant tones of yellow, orange, purple, and blue.
I remember the sparkle they left in my heart
and the lovely inspiration they did impart
as we played with them on summer nights.
They danced and floated, twinkling their graceful
    lights.
I completely took it for granted, at that tender young
    age, that things aren't always what they seem.
As an adult, it occurred to me that lightning bugs only
    come in yellow and green.
Wondering if my memory served me correctly, I asked
    my sisters, to be sure.
"When you were a child, outside at night, do you
    remember what color the fireflies were?"
They took on a far-away gaze, lost in the memories of
    our yesterdays.
They answered fondly, "Of course, we recall the hues!
    They were different colors of yellow, orange,
    purple, and blue!"
Feeling better about my mind, I'm now faced with a
    new query: Were they fireflies at all, or do children
    see fairies?

— COLLEEN COFFMAN

FOREWORD

Inside these pages, you will find an assortment of fun images and the intriguing stories behind them. While this book is completely inspired by and dedicated to my friends, the Faeries, it's also a very candid look through a window into my life, odd and amusing as it has been (and continues to be).

You see, I'm an intuitive. I see, hear and feel things most people either can't or refuse to. This diary is based on my relationship with exactly that. You don't have to believe me, and you don't have to believe in Faeries to appreciate the wonder, education, beauty, and magic they've brought into my world. I spent many years pouring my mind, heart, experience, and soul into this diary.

The title, "Adventures of a Sketch Diary" is meaningful on multiple levels: It's a visual record of some of my most interesting encounters and experiences, and the book itself enjoyed adventures I can only speculate about–the likes of which began in February of 2012.

Then, as lives tend to do on occasion, mine decided to spin into a regulation shit storm. There was a divorce, a few moves, and my storage unit was burglarized by drug addicts, who stole many precious items that were meaningful only to me and mine. It was in the midst of all that chaos my treasured diary went missing. I was heartbroken at this huge loss and assumed it was lost forever. Sad as I was though, I still had a few low-resolution photos from it which I cherished deeply.

Cut to June 2020. I was house and pet-sitting for a friend while she was out of town. A little after dusk, I sat in the backyard having a smoke while the dogs played, and I was enjoying the hundreds of fireflies lighting up the lush, spring night. It made me think of a time when I watched the Faeries dance in the nightfall. I missed them terribly, but I hadn't been able to settle down long enough to connect in many years. At that point, I did some meditating on those good 'ole days. It brought me comfort and made me smile.

So, you can well imagine my surprise when the next day, completely out of the blue, I received a random message from a young man I hadn't heard from since 2014. He said he had my sketch diary and would like to return it. I almost fell over.

I went the following day and picked it up from him, crying with joy. My long, lost friend had come home! I'm still not quite sure how it fell into that young man's hands, but it did. Why did it take over six years for him to return it, and why was he so compelled? I don't know.

This sketch diary is full of my Faerie sketches. Isn't it a tad more than coincidence that I was focused on these wonderful friends just the night before, for the first time in many years? In all my life of experience, I've concluded there is no such thing as coincidence. I fully accept that the Faeries and I reconnected that night, and it delights me to the core.

With that, and at the insistence of my family, I decided to finish the diary and share it. I've printed these drawings as they were in my sketch diary, including all the scribbles, mistakes, and notes. I tried several methods of capturing the images, but photos and scans simply don't do the drawings justice. Some of the drawings came out a little light but have been adjusted for brightness and contrast.

This is such a great adventure; after all, the sketches are fun, but the story is the stuff dreams are made of. So, without further ado, welcome to my strange and magical world!

Faeries E'Such

THE BARN

My mom and dad got this sketch diary for me on my birthday. I don't recall which year, but I think it was 2000-ish. At that time, I was traveling all over the United States as a professional airbrush artist, special effects, makeup artist, and body painter, all the while being a wife and the mother of four awesome boys. So, I was on the road a lot and this sketch diary kept me company on some long, lonely trips.

When I wasn't traveling, family time was a priority, and we spent a lot of that time together at *the barn*. The barn was about 50 acres of land on the south side of Kansas City, Missouri that we took care of for a local elderly couple who were friends of my then-husband. It was like an unknown oasis with a patch of timber, a lot of pasture, a small pond, a big pole barn and a small horse barn.

We built a stone spit in a two-acre yard next to the horse barn and we spent a lot of quality time there enjoying the grounds, cooking on an open fire, roasting marshmallows and lighting fireworks.

At the beginning of this story, my ex-husband was a mechanic, and he used the big pole barn as a storage space for dozens of parts cars. He took this out in trade for being the caretaker of this property. We spent countless hours mowing, maintaining and generally keeping an eye on things and it was a good trade for all of us until someone started vandalizing the cars. Once that started, it continued almost daily for way too long. For weeks, we would walk the boundaries of the barn at all hours of the day and night, hoping to catch whoever was smashing windows and tearing up the cars.

It was on one of these twilight walks, that as my ex-husband and I stopped to take a break against the back fence line, we noticed some glowing, orange orbs in a bush growing out of the fence. They were about the size and color of softly lit cigar cherries, but there wasn't any smoke or smell.

Upon closer inspection, we found the bush was absolutely full of them, but we couldn't figure out what they were. Fungus, maybe? Optical illusion? The more we looked, the more we found, but it was getting dark enough, we just couldn't tell exactly what they were.

The next morning, we went back to investigate in the daylight and couldn't find anything that even remotely resembled what we had seen. It was just a bush with no discerning or remarkable qualities. There were no seed pods, bulging branches, fungus, or, for that matter, anything at all that could account for what we had seen the night before.

It made us scratch our heads, but at that moment we had more important fish to fry, so we let it go and went on about our business of trying to catch the idiots destroying our property.

It was a short time after that when we came across a giant Faerie ring in the middle of the field. It was composed of several dozen extra-large mushrooms and was every bit of 20' or more in diameter. Then, we started seeing a lot of lights zooming to and fro, all over the property. At first, they were mostly little white balls of light, about the size of golf balls, zipping through the field at night.

But it wasn't long before those lights evolved into colorful orbs and started making an assortment of sounds. They were even apparent to people who didn't believe in the paranormal at all, who were seeing them without any influence from the rest of us.

Through all of this, it became obvious and indisputable that we were all being accepted and included in the lives of the property's resident Faeries.

Now, my whole life I've been able to peek through the veil to see and hear ghosts, specters and entities. I even spent several years as a professional "psychic" (I hate that word!) and many decades as a paranormal investigator (which I still engage in every chance I get), but I had never had such close contact with Fae before. I had no idea what they were about, beyond the fairy tales we all grew up with.

Fortunately, I was honored with a crash course that started at the barn, which, as you'll see, is the locale for a number of the stories and sketches in this diary.

The Fairies began coming to me at home, in dreams, in visions, and in meditation. They were sweet, beautiful, kind, and curious. The manifestations became so physical, our cats would chase the little lights through the house, playing with them and really freaking us all out.

It was a very natural decision to dedicate my sketch diary to the Faeries, drawing each one as they presented themselves to me. This is where the artwork begins. I'll share with you everything they are to me - the good, the bad and the ugly.

Speaking of ugly, a little something to remember during this journey: Just because something looks unpleasant or frightening by your standards doesn't mean it's a bad guy. Love and beauty come in all types of packages. Oh, and we did finally catch the vandals red-handed. It was a group of kids about 13 years old who thought the cars were fair game since they never saw anyone around them. I wanted to spank them, and throat-punch their parents...but that's a story for another day.

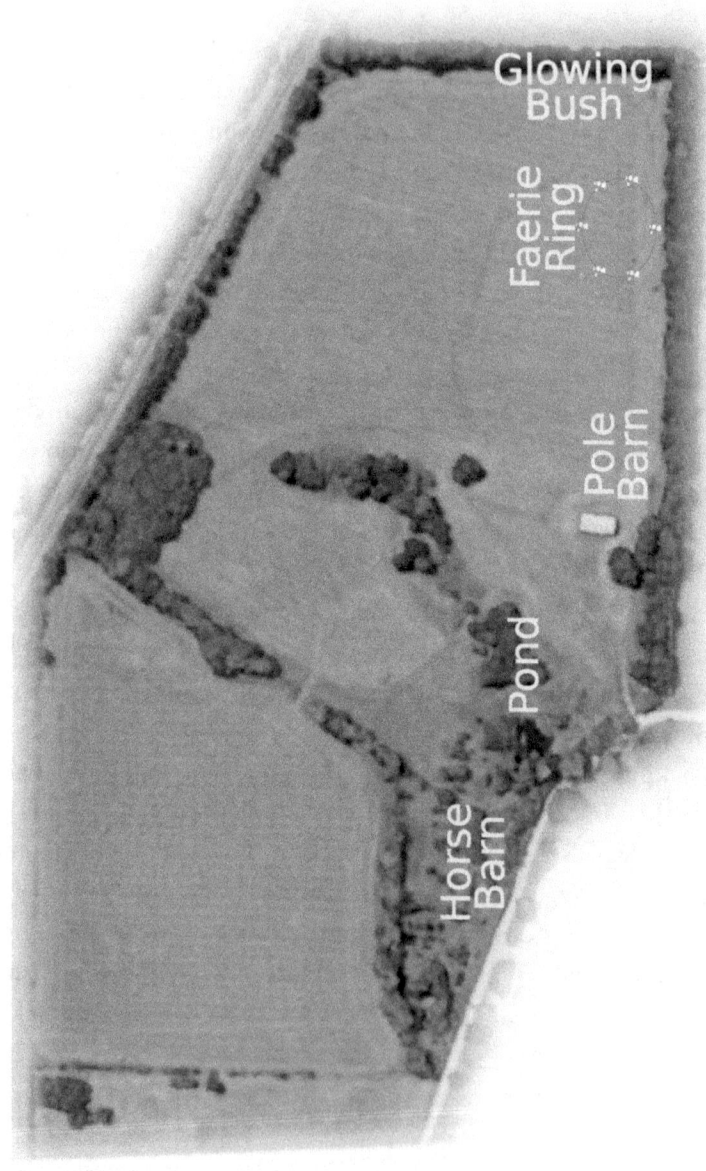

Aerial Image of the barn, showing the field, pole barn, horse barn, pond, Faerie ring, and glowing bush.

ROOT

At first, the visuals were coming at me so fast, I almost felt as if they were pelting me, and it was hard to keep up. You see, most Faeries tend to be nimble and super speedy, and they don't slow down for much. Add to this that they can be so easily distracted; it's just the way they're built. So, it's hard on them to hold still long enough for me to draw them. It's kind of like asking a lightning bolt to stop and chat over a cup of coffee.

It was maddening to see something I wanted to get on paper, but it was moving so quickly that it was a challenge to get a good grip on the details. That's when I turned to my Spirit Guides for advice.

Yes, I have voices in my head, and I communicate with them daily. I call them my Guides, for lack of a better term. They advise me on everything, and their advice is golden. They have never steered me wrong, even when I doubted them, and they are always with me, even when I thought they weren't. Some people call them guardian angels, while others say it's the voice of God or the Creator. For all I know, they're aliens or dimensional beings, but I think it's probable they are all of the above. The truth is, they've always been a part of my life and I take great joy in that. There are so many, I have no idea what their names are, but I do my best to listen when they speak.

They told me to "root". They said that by rooting, I would be able to sort out where to start. They defined this as sitting quietly in a grassy area and meditating on being one with our planet. This process would still me and connect me with the Earth's vibration. Since Faeries are integral with that particular energy, this would give me the quiet I needed to accomplish my goal.

Because I traveled so much and I had four young boys at home, I wasn't able to find the time or grassy area, but I improvised and took advantage of my quiet time in the air instead; at an altitude of 30,000 feet, traveling on a plane, I started this very busy sketch I've titled *Root*.

Root is a montage of many Fae who were running through my world in the beginning. The original image is an ink drawing depicting the commonalities shared by the Fae (and which should be shared by all of us) with our Earth.

The second image is a painted/airbrushed reproduction on a much larger scale that was commissioned to hang in a client's home shortly after my diary was recovered. This creation also shows the light orbs we were starting to see regularly, many of which we captured with our cameras (more on orbs later). Funny thing: When I completed this canvas, I posted it on social media. It made me giggle that Facebook tried to tag the faces in the orbs.

Root: Original Ink sketch

Root: Airbrush/hand brush reproduction

NAGA

The Faeries often told me they were sad about humans. According to them, in the beginning, human beings and Faerie Folk all shared the responsibility of being stewards of our Earth. Instead of staying on this path, we were distracted away from our agreement by the pursuit of material comforts and technology, leaving them to care for the planet–an undertaking which continues to become ever more daunting, as our selfish, careless, and destructive behaviors intensify.

That's why they slid into the hidden obscurity of their own realm, not wanting to interact with people. Some Faeries are more than a little bitter about this and most of them are very impatient with the arrogant abandon we practice when it comes to nature.

We talked about a lot of things together, the Faeries and me. For instance, roadkill really bothers them. They don't understand why life is so disposable to people. They fervently believe all life is dear and death should be honored, whether it's human or beast. They tried to convince me that a dead animal on the road should be scraped up and returned to the Earth naturally, whether buried or given to the carrion eaters. While my heart is with them there, I had to remind them that I didn't want to be the next body on the road, either. So, they'd have to accept a quick prayer for the animal instead of me dodging traffic to remove a carcass. We revisited this same conversation every time there was a dead animal on the road for the longest time, but in the end, they grudgingly understood and agreed.

Faeries are a hard sell when it comes to human beings, but they do recognize that there are other entities and energies affecting our planet; wicked usurpers, who knowingly corrupt our bodies, minds, and spirits. Some of these beings have been here for thousands of years, manipulating and enslaving our race, raping our natural resources, and brutalizing our spirits. They whisper dark intent into our ears while sculpting our society to serve them and their evil, narcissistic psyches. They disguise themselves as celebrity personalities, as our leaders in government and organized religion, and they use all forms of media to lull us into their maniacal, scandalous conspiracies.

It is because of these diabolical influences that the Fae find patience with us and are more likely to hide from or ignore humans than to engage us with their anger or frustrations. Make no mistake, Faeries can be mischievous, malicious, and downright dangerous when their patience wears out, and really, who can blame them? But they will also respond with beauty and kindness when and where they see fit, and they have a high measure of respect for people who treat nature with love and care.

Naga is an ink drawing embodiment of the things the Faeries told me about these malevolent creatures. The word "Naga" is a Sanskrit word referring to the shape-shifting serpent people found in Hindu, Buddhist, and Jainism lore. According to myth, not all of them are bad guys, but the ones who are, are *really* bad.

I thought this drawing came out to look a lot like Joe Camel, but hey, they're shape-shifters... right? At the time I created this, the Fae told me these shape-shifting dick weeds were in their 11th hour on our planet, meaning they were being forced to leave our reality. They spoke these words to me shortly after the 9-11 terrorist attacks on the U.S.A., and while I could see the writing on the wall, I couldn't see the light at the end of the tunnel.

The Faeries felt the crushing grief cast over the World and were trying to lend a bit of comfort, as I had been in the Twin Towers only 2 weeks before they fell. In fact, my last night in New York gave me the worst nightmare I've ever had, which included watching the choking smoke permeate my sleeping mind. I worked with several people who died in the tragedy, and it was really quite a mind fuck for me.

I went to my mother about this. She talked about critical mass and said she believed when people finally woke up, it was going to happen all at once. We would join our hearts together and these sinister bastards would be forced to loosen their grip, allowing us our freedom. At the time, I could feel it coming, but it was so far away.

Now, as I write this book (August of 2020), I see this awareness suddenly soaking into every soul I encounter. Humans are slamming awake all over the World, and while it's quite a tribulation to wake up in the middle of a major clusterfuck, I finally see what my mother and the Faeries were talking about. Critical mass has been activated. Yay for us, now is our time to be free and evolve!

Naga: Ink sketch

TROLL OF THE RED SHED

The only other structure on the barn property was a little, red, wooden shed, almost completely hidden by overgrowth. It wasn't used for much because it wasn't a very friendly or convenient place, but they sometimes stored hay, tack supplies, and feed in it, as the property owners occasionally rented the pasture for horses.

Whenever this building was approached, especially after dark, strange noises would almost always frighten people away, and my kids steered completely clear of the place, day or night.

While I was mowing around it one day, I caught a glance of the cranky guy who had taken up residence in the shed. It was only a murky glimpse and trying to get closer to him for a better look was super uncomfortable. Instead, I took out my trusty sketch diary, sat on a rock a few feet away and started to draw. The more I drew, the more I could see, although he stayed deep in the shadows at best. I gave him privacy, but he did poke his head out just enough for me to create "Troll of the Red Shed".

While he appears to be quite frightful, the truth is, they all have their own personalities and some of them are just grumpy shut-ins. So, it's always a good idea to follow your gut and approach Fae with polite regard. Even a sour puss will reflect respect.

Troll of the Red Shed: Pencil sketch

YOUNG DRYAD

There were a lot of cool and interesting trees on the barn property, a great many of them being Hawthorns and Hedge Apples (which were a real challenge to mow and drive around).

The Hedge Apple trees mostly lined the fence row, mangling any mower blade unlucky enough to find them, and the Hawthorns populated much of the timber found in the back corner.

If you're unfamiliar, Hawthorns put off thorns long and strong enough to puncture a tire, and we had our fair share of flats because of them. I've actually put a thorn clear through a sandal and into my foot, just by stepping on it at the wrong angle–all of this to say, while those ornery trees gave us a run for our money, there were also a few groves of the kinder Cottonwoods, Elms, Oaks, Weeping Willows and Sycamore trees.

One day, while walking through one of those little oak groves, I saw some movement in a young tree not far from me. Being nearsighted and not wearing my glasses, I thought it was a snake to begin with because it looked like the bark was moving.

Then I moved closer for a better view and met a real beauty. She was young with sparkling eyes, and she appeared to be part of the tree as she moved through the trunk, bark and branches.

I did a quick draft sketch of her, then I had to go home and research what she was. I learned she was a tree spirit known as a Dryad, and she took care of the whole grove of trees around her.

It saddens me that I didn't get more time with her before we lost access to the barn, but I'm hopeful that I'll get a chance to go back someday and see how much her grove has grown.

Young Dryad: Pencil sketch

PRINCESS OF THE POND

As I mentioned in *The Barn* chapter, there was also a small pond on the property. It was a very serene place, surrounded by Cottonwood and Weeping Willow trees with only one, small footpath to lead you through the trees.

I spent a lot of time there with my young boys, catching and releasing little sun perch and just sitting on the banks enjoying the vibe. I recall wondering if it was spring fed or if it stayed full because it was at a good place to catch the drain-off. I'm going to presume the latter though because it was super muddy. We never swam there because we couldn't see what might be hiding in it and didn't know how deep it was, but I can tell you it was deep enough that I never saw it go dry.

While sitting on the bank one still, summer afternoon, I saw a stir in the water that was obviously too big for a sun perch. The disturbance startled me and put my senses into overdrive.

Suddenly, I could see in my mind's eye, a little water nymph or mermaid of sorts, peering out of the water at me. That's frequently how it is with the Faeries; you don't always see them with your eyes, but more often with your heart and mind.

When I turned my gaze in her direction, she popped her head

back under the surface, causing a bloop and ruffle in the water. I pulled out my trusty sketch diary and drafted a quick outline to be completed later.

I'll tell you; I saw a lot of weird things around that pond, but it was peaceful and pretty at the heart. In fact, I was never uncomfortable being there, day or night, even when witnessing the strangest of sights.

Here's a crazy example: One time my kids and I saw a bird there that can only be described as a pterodactyl of some sort.

It was a huge, gray-feathered bird, sitting in a treetop on the opposite side of the pond from us, about 50 feet away. Now, before you assume we must've been hallucinating, the reason we came to be there in the first place was to investigate a shrill, strange, unfamiliar screeching.

The bird's wings were feathered but shaped more like a bat than a bird. It had a large, predatory beak and a massive, bony crest on the top of its head. I've searched every bird species in the world and the only thing that even came close (but not really), was the cassowary from New Guinea.

In the weeks and months that followed, many people saw the strange bird in the area. To the best of my knowledge, it simply disappeared without anyone ever identifying what it was. I only wish I would've drawn it then and could include it here, but I didn't.

There were also many orb pictures taken around that pond. I know, I know... orbs are all dust, moisture and pollen. Right? Well, I beg to differ there. I agree that some are certainly small particles, insects, or reflections, but others have very distinct faces, colors and interesting patterns, too. I could write a book about that. Maybe another time.

My point is, this World is filled with things we don't understand, and keeping an open mind is the best path to new knowledge and fresh wonders.

Princess of the Pond: Pencil sketch

DARK FAERIE

Growing up, my parents were always incredibly supportive of my strange ways. From an early age, I seemed to know things I had no earthly way of knowing and they never once made me feel like a freak for it. In fact, they figured out the best way to deal with me was to nurture my weirdness.

Thank you, Mom and Dad! It turned out those talents serve me very well in my adult life, and I'm not insecure about them in the least. I tried very hard to pay that forward to my own children when they were young; if one of my boys was frightened of the monster under the bed, we'd go together and tell it to get out of our house. I never chastised them, told them it was their imagination, or attempted to rationalize it away, because I knew better.

I think most people would be genuinely surprised and perhaps even terrified to know that children really do see things adults can't (or more accurately, won't).

There were many times entities would follow us home from the barn. While they were mostly pleasant to deal with, sometimes they were not, as in the case of my son's experience with a "Dark Faerie."

When my youngest son was about four years old, he had a bad dream that woke him up shaking and crying from a day nap. I was working from home that day and my sister was there with us. Poor little guy was terribly upset. He told us that there was this dark lady inside the wall, who was taunting and threatening him from a hole in the sheetrock next to his bed. He said she was really mad, and that she was looking for something that resembled a black marble, which she called her looking glass.

My sister and I went into his room to investigate further. We looked down into the hole thinking it might be a mouse scratching around but found nothing except a dark vibe in the room.

My son flatly refused to go back into his bedroom, so I sat and drew his dark lady as he described her, which seemed to ease his fear. Although I never saw this one, I sure felt something, as did everyone else there that day. Interestingly, and this was not the only time this has happened, once I drew her, the uncomfortable energy subsided (and my little boy seemed to forget all about her).

Dark Faerie: Ink sketch

THE EYES

S trange things pass through my brain when I give it free rein to wander. Sometimes they're good things, sometimes they're bad things, and sometimes they are completely random, but most are always strange. There are times I let them go, times I hold them tight, and other times they don't seem to make any sense at all. Most often though, those messages and visions that originally made absolutely no sense will suddenly come back to me during a certain moment or situation, and then it clicks in place and makes perfect sense.

The Eye is one of those things that really didn't make sense when it first appeared in my mind. I knew it was important because it kept popping in at very haphazard times. I assumed it was referring to the Eye of Ra or the Eye of Horus.

So, I did a little ink drawing to help me focus on the message. It turned out this went much deeper and I was seeing the actual physiology of an eye, but not eyes as we know them. These eyes belonged to something inhuman but could appear like a human.

In later years, I found it interesting when the Reptoids, Draconians and black-eyed children appeared on the scene, as well as some political, religious and famous figures who had completely black eyeballs in photos and videos. Look 'em up. They're pretty creepy and it made me wonder...

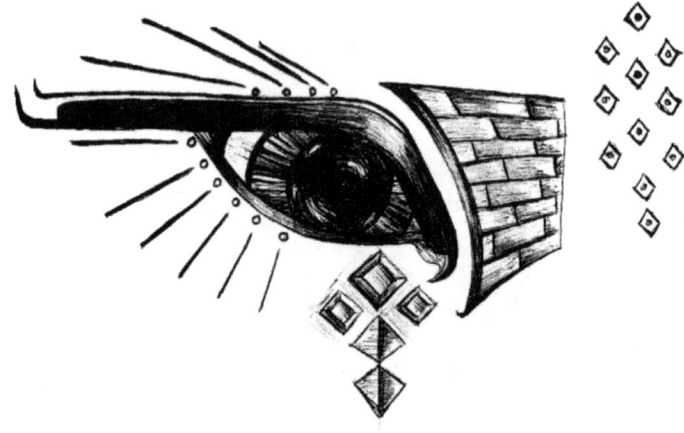

Eye of Ra: Ink sketch

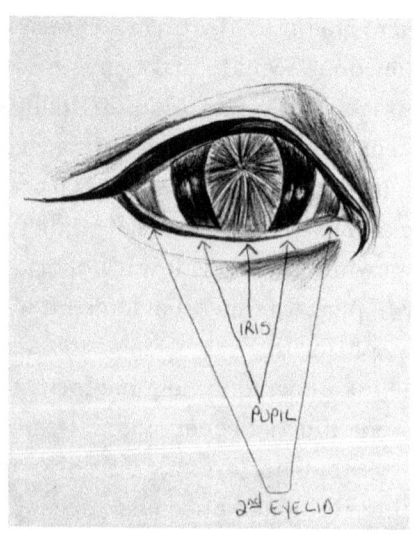

Anatomy of a Black Eye: Ink sketch

TAITIN THE SYLPH

This is a chapter that's very near and dear to my heart. Remember when I talked about the white lights that would zip through the field at the barn? Well, when they started changing colors and making sounds, they also took on a mental form for me. By that, I mean I could see them in my mind's eye.

You could see the lights with your physical eyes, and they were most commonly white, electric blue, and plasma purple in color. Many saw them that way, and the sounds they made were audible to everyone. They made noises ranging from high-pitched buzzing to whooshes, ringing, trilling, and even low bleating like that of a goat.

However, in my mind's eye, I could see their little bodies, the likeness of which I've drawn in this book. One little purple light really bonded with me. I called her Taitin and she most resembled what I found to be a Sylph.

Taitin was a beauty. She had long, flowing hair that she loved to style into different looks, even though she usually kept at least part of it down. Her huge and mesmerizing eyes were almost too big for her tiny, delicate face. It was hard to tell what her clothes looked like because her body was glowing so brightly it was hard to see. Her form was thin and willowy, although I could never see any definition to her hands or feet. They appeared to just fade out, like mist. She made a high-pitched trilling sound that would almost tickle my ear. Others compared the sound to a cordless phone. She had such high energy, constantly chattering and moving around quickly, but she was so warm and compassionate about life and this world.

Taitin must have been a little Faerie encyclopedia or gossip columnist, the way she would regale me with tales from her world and share details about the other Faeries. Allow me to share a couple of examples.

She's the one who told me that the ring of mushrooms we call a Faerie ring is only a 3rd-dimensional representation of a real Faerie ring. "The real ones glow," she said.

She told me about Gremlins and how to deal with them when my ex-husband lost his big set of keys.

"They're really just little scientists and need something to keep them busy. So, when you're bothered by Gremlins, ask them to fix or find things instead of break or steal them," she told me.

Shortly after I asked the Gremlins to help find his keys, they appeared at the barn on top of a tall fence post next to the entry gate. I don't know if they took them to begin with or went out and found them. Either way, I thanked them for returning them.

I learned so much from Taitin and call her my friend. I drew a lot of this sweet girl, in part because I dealt most closely with her. She was the one who would follow me home and play with the cats. I don't think any of us ever completely became accustomed to seeing a fast-moving purple light flying around a corner, followed by a cat who was on it like a laser. There were so many nights I would lie awake as she flitted through my room, bright and beautiful and completely distracting me from slumber.

Taitin is the only one we were ever fortunate enough to photograph, a copy of which I've included in this chapter. I know you can't see the color of her glow in the black-and-white print (if you're looking at the print version), but you can definitely see a purple halo around her. This image is very much the way I always saw her, except I could see more detail.

So...all the images in this chapter are of Taitin and the Sylphs (sounds like a punk rock group). I sure love and miss you, girl.

The following images are an assortment of Sylphs I've encountered at the barn and many other places, with the last few being Taitin herself.

Sylphs: Ink sketch with notes

The Family Sylph: Ink sketch

Relax with the Faeries: Ink sketch

Shy Sylph: Ink sketch

Small Sylph: Ink sketch

Little Sylph: Ink sketch

Taitin the Sylph: Ink sketch

In this portrait of Taitin, I didn't fully capture her body, but I think it's a rather good likeness. I actually intended to have this image tattooed on my shoulder until my kids said it looked like the Nanny. They were just teasing me, but it put a bad taste in my mouth for using it as a tattoo.

After Taitin entered my life, she told me her kind was all over the world and I could interact with them, no matter where I was. I took her advice and searched for them in every place I traveled. To my delight, she was right; Sylphs are everywhere, and like humans, they each have unique personalities and physical characteristics.

These tiny beauties have always been a joy to deal with, giving me insight into the local news, geology and general vibe of the area. I've only been to two places where they were out of balance; those I encountered in the Denver, CO area were skittish to the point of being frightened. It made me sad and suspicious to think about what was going on there that would cause them to be so. The other area was the Midland/Odessa, TX region. There, they were sick, sad and almost rogue. It kind of reminded me of a Faerie Mad Max. My gut tells me the reason for this is due to the hundreds of square miles of land that have been used, abused and raped by the oil industry. It stands to reason that the health of the land has a direct effect on all the beings (including the Fae!) who live there. This particular region is a great example; it's so fraught with illness caused by the molestation of oil rigs, refinery stacks belching black smoke and abandoned petrol factories, it has made the Faeries sick–another fine example of how human beings have turned our backs on our commitment to being the earth's stewards, in favor of our material aspirations.

Taitin the Sylph: Pencil sketch

As I mentioned earlier in this chapter, we caught what we believe to be Taitin the Sylph on camera. Here is that photo, taken during one of many family gatherings we held at the barn. I've blurred some faces, but that's the only edit on this full image. If you look in the top/left corner of the picture, you can see a tiny light hanging over my head (I'm crouched over the fire with my youngest son, tending the chicken we were cooking for supper).

This is exactly what she looked like to all of us on the numerous occasions we saw her flying through the night, only she was a more vivid shade of purple. My dad took this photo on his Olympus digital camera but didn't see the anomaly until he loaded the card onto his computer. The images following the original are cropped, enlarged and/or adjusted for brightness and contrast to enable you to better see her.

Original Photo of Possible Sylph by Johnnie Coffman.

*Photo of a possible Sylph, cropped and adjusted for
brightness/contrast.*

Original image, cropped and adjusted for brightness & contrast to show anomaly.

Photo of a possible Sylph, cropped, enlarged and adjusted for brightness/contrast.

SATYRS

It used to be when I thought of Satyrs, I envisioned creatures from Greek Mythology, half human/half goat, or the cartoon version found in Disney's Fantasia. My experiences at the barn showed me a whole different side of these beings.

Honestly, I had chalked them up to being wholly fantasy before I met one dancing around the barnyard, and I heard him before I saw him. I never encountered him in the daytime, either. He was nocturnal, only making an appearance after the sun was fully set, and he had a real penchant for pretty girls. He bleated just like a sheep or goat, often playing with your hair as he passed by; or he'd caress you on the shoulder, back, or butt.

He moved very quickly, seen usually as a blur in the night. It took me a while to get a clear enough look at him to see what he was, much less be able to draw him. Once I got a grip on his physical appearance, I did several works dedicated to him.

I called him Osma and I never was able to really talk directly with him. He loved to dance and leap like a ballet dancer under the moon, but I didn't ever see him play a flute as they're depicted in most art you see. Maybe that's an individual choice or talent? I don't know, but I sure enjoyed watching him interact with the ladies who came to the barn. I can't count the number of times one of these females would tell me that something touched them on the butt, or they heard a goat before something caressed their hair.

Osma the Satyr: Ink sketch

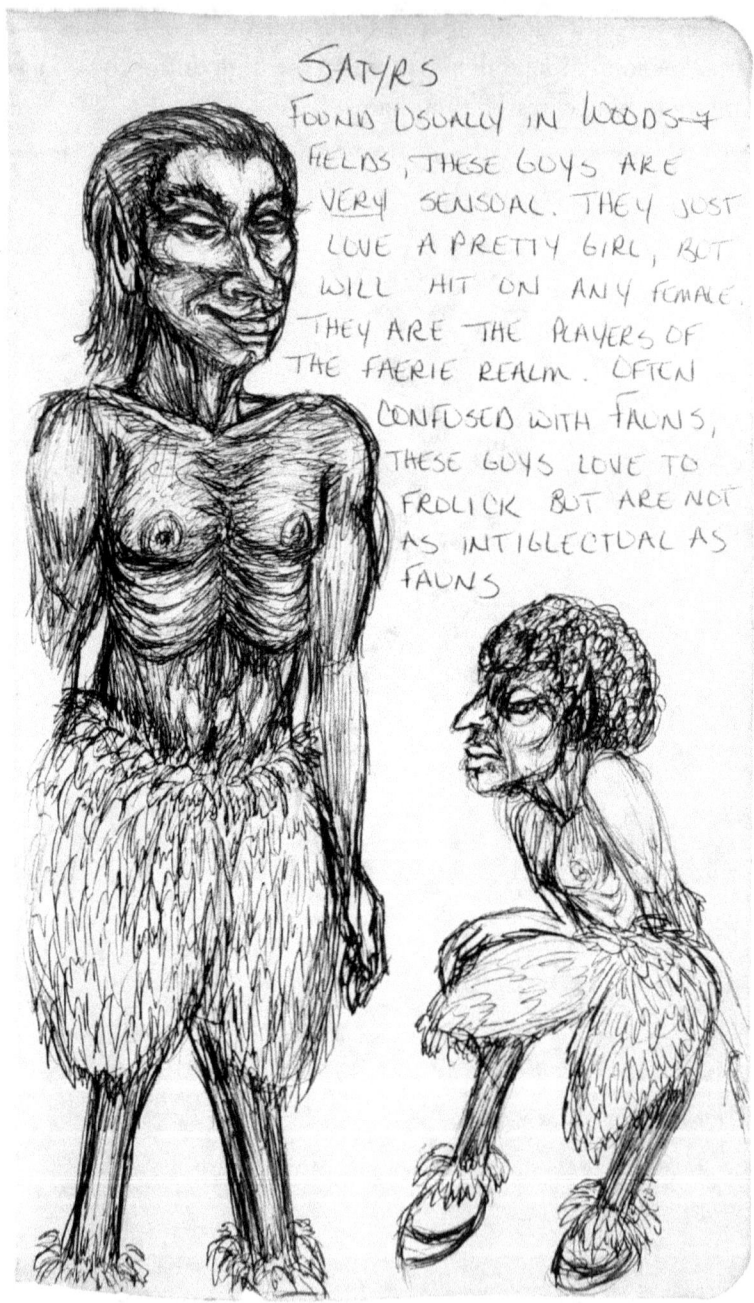

Satyrs: Ink sketch with notes

Osma the Satyr: Airbrush painting

AYRE SPRINGS & THE WEATHER SPRITES

Being on airplanes as much as I was, I spent a lot of time gazing out the windows. One day, as I was cloud-watching at 30,000 feet, I noticed beautiful, tiny, sparkling lights in the sky around us. They weren't inside the cabin and we weren't flying through bad weather yet, but the clouds were thickly building into a wicked storm.

Almost as soon as I noticed the little lights, one of them spoke to me. She called herself an Ayre Spring, explaining she and others like her were responsible for clouds and precipitation. She said, in a world where the weather occurred naturally, they rode the air, supervising the clouds, rain and snow.

I was intrigued by her use of the phrase "naturally occurring," so I asked her to expand. She said there were weather patterns being influenced by humans and that the Ayre Springs rarely had control over those situations. I asked if that had to do with global warming, cooling, or pollution. She said no, none of these. The unnatural weather patterns were created by machines playing around with our upper atmosphere.

After much research, I discovered these manipulated weather conditions probably have a lot to do with the HAARP project in Alaska and top secret "cloud seeding" projects. At the time, these anomalies were referred to as "chem-trails" and had been labeled as a conspiracy theory. As a matter of fact, only a few years ago did the US military come out and admit to cloud seeding, which has really been going on since the early 80s.

Now, when I hear the term "conspiracy theory", I've learned I should investigate further because it most likely has some truth to it that the assholes in control don't want us to know about.

These sketches represent several weather related Fae I've met along the way. Some of them are easy to talk to and some of them are impossibly turbulent and completely beyond communicating.

AYRE SPRINGS

REMINDING ME OF
SMALLER, ROUNDER
SYLPHS, THEY ARE
EXPERIENCED AS/WITH
DEW + RAINDROPS.
NOT QUITE AIR FAE, +
NOT QUITE WATERFAE,
THEY ARE ACTUALLY BOTH.
FIRST MET IN COLUMBUS, OH,
SEEN AS SMALL, WHITE
PINPOINTS OF LIGHT.

Ayre Springs: Ink sketch with notes

Dirt Devil: Ink sketch

Ocean of the Air: Ink sketch

Rainbow Storm: Pencil sketch

RANDOM PERSONALITIES

O ver the years, I've found so many Faerie types, it's crazy to think about. Some are part of a larger whole or group, some are rare but still have others like them, and others are completely unique. Often, I'm surprised by how much they resemble the Fae of folklore, mythos and fairy tales, and I'm sometimes taken aback by the ways their physical attributes have been misunderstood to be something they're not. Take for example the Gnomes (also known as Tomte or Nisse in Nordic myths and Duende in Mexico and South America). Legends represent them wearing tall hats when, in reality, their heads are really tall and the hats they wear are simply covering their massive beans. The images in this chapter are all about the random Fae I've found all over the US.

The Alchemist: Ink sketch–The symbols are alchemic for Earth, Air, Fire, Water, Sun, Moon, Venus, Mercury, Saturn, Mars & Jupiter.

A little nymph called All Ears: Ink sketch

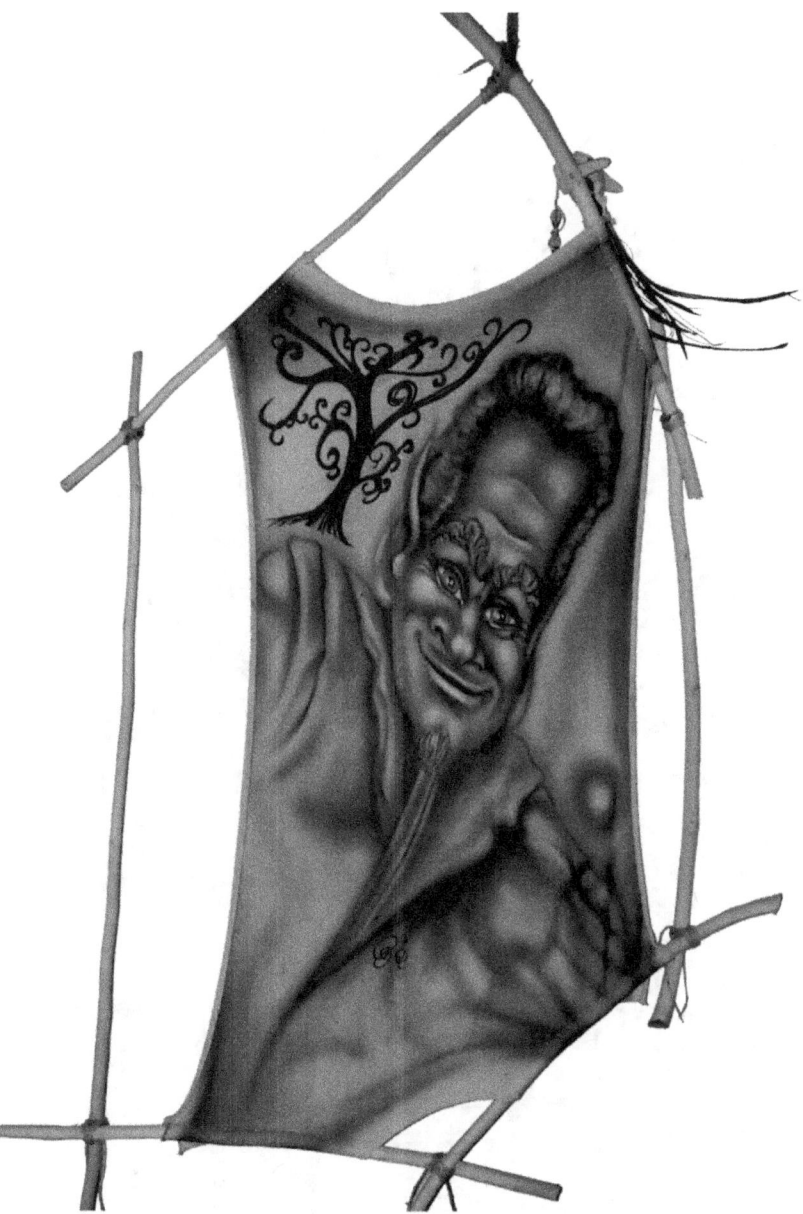

Homer the Mulberry Gnome: Airbrush painting in Mulberry branch frame

Little Bird: Ink sketch

Muse and More: Ink sketch

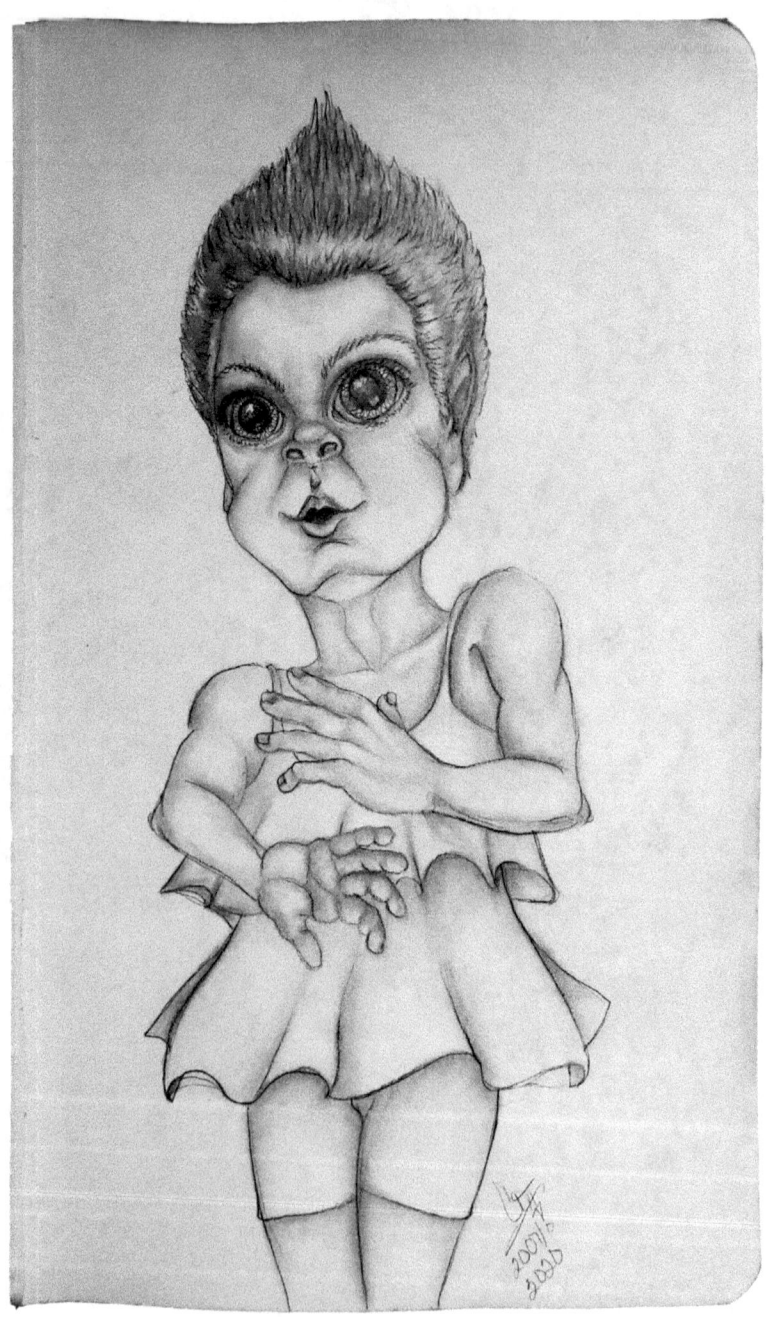

Sprite Surprised: Pencil sketch

Wood Grain Faerie: Ink sketch

"Trolls" ink pen sketch with notes.

LADY OF THE WOODS

O ne of my favorite ladies EVER! I met this enchanting sentinel of the woods while I was on a job in northeastern Ohio at the scenic and mystical Nelson Ledges.

What a story this is! In 2003, I was hired to do makeup and face painting for the rap group, Insane Clown Posse, at their annual Gathering of the Juggalos. I took a team of artists to Cleveland for the 4-day music festival, which we were fortunate to work for three years in a row. We all agree even now that these were some of the best times of our lives (despite the fact they still owe me $500 from the last year)! We painted evil clown faces on thousands of ICP fans (AKA the Juggalos), and each year, we were more and more amazed by the magic of Nelson Ledges.

Nelson Ledges is located outside of Cleveland and occupies about 250 acres of stunningly beautiful land. The ancient trees form a canopy so high, it's like visiting another world. The forest is rich with wildlife everywhere you look, and the general vibe is full of peace and charm.

The grounds are so expansive, we didn't really notice anything strange the first year, except we were constantly encountering groups of Juggalos who were desperately lost. It happened a lot, mostly after dark, but we chalked it up to excessive partying in a giant forest and we giggled about it frequently. One night, our second year of working the Gathering, we decided to take our group out into the campgrounds to enjoy the forest after we had finished with our workday. It was purely delightful everywhere we went, and we were completely mesmerized.

There was no electricity in the campground, but that didn't stop the Juggalos from creating one of the coolest experiences ever. It was like being in Lothlorien on Juggalo steroids.

While we were wandering around, listening to the woop-woops and Dave Chapelle impersonations ("What? Ok...!" or "Fuck yo coffee table!"), I saw a circle of glowing blue mushrooms on the path a few feet ahead of us. Almost as soon as I saw it, it disappeared. It occurred to me that I had just seen a Faerie ring... a *real* Faerie ring like Taitin had told me about!

Then, I heard my sister say "Where the hell are we? This doesn't look familiar at all." The rest of us stopped, joking lightly about being lost. Then the confusion set in. There were five of us, we weren't drinking, and none of us knew where we were. We poured over our map of the camp, but nothing made sense.

So, we wandered bewildered and aimlessly until we saw a staff member on a golf cart ahead. We stopped, asking for help, and he just laughed. As it turned out, getting lost in this forest was such a common thing, even with the people who worked there, that employees weren't allowed into the campgrounds without a radio. It was a regular occurrence, especially after dark, for staff to lose their way through the forest and need someone to come and get them back on track. He said it happened to him, finding himself on the opposite side of the forest from where he thought he was. He jokingly said that the paths were constantly moving, so you never knew where you'd end up. Or maybe he wasn't saying it in jest after all...Made me wonder about Faerie rings and just how real they are.

During the day, while we were working, we listened to the Juggalos tell stories about the woods. One such story came from an ICP staff member who decided he needed a bit of meditation on his break. He said he was in the middle of the lake about dusk, marinating on a big rock, when he felt a mosquito land on his forehead. He didn't really want to move, but just as he was ready to slap the bloodsucker, he felt a soft whish against his face. He opened his eyes just in time to see a bat floating away from him. He said he sat on that rock way past his break, watching the bats scoop mosquitos off him.

It was at this same lake where I caught the presence of the Lady of the Woods. That night, she came to my dreams and I could feel her strong, gentle presence all through the forest. She said she took care of the forest and all who lived there. She was so beautiful! Someday, I hope to go back to Nelson Ledges without all the people around and do some marinating of my own.

Lady of the Woods: Ink sketch

CHAKRA FAERIE

All of us have Guides, whether you realize it or not. Some are with us for life, and some make a temporary appearance but leave after their mission is accomplished; some are loved ones who've passed over; and some may even be from past lives.

This sweet and sassy lady came to me in my dreams. She said she was there to help me adjust my chakras and balance my Merkabah.

For those of you who're unfamiliar with chakras, they are the energy centers found throughout the body. There are seven major chakras, each concentrated in a gland or organ. They're arranged like this: top of the head/pituitary gland, forehead/pineal gland, throat/thyroid gland, chest/heart, belly/solar plexus, sacral/sex glands, and root/coxal gland. For thousands of years, mystics all over the World have worked to nurture these energy centers, promoting healing and well-being.

The Merkabah is a little more complicated, but it has a direct relation to the chakras. It has been described as an energy vehicle or conduit, used by ascended masters to connect with those in tune with higher realms. The ancients described them as appearing like two pyramids on top of each other, the top one pointing down and the bottom one pointing up.

This lovely lady was around just long enough for me to wrap my head around these teachings, then she was gone. I never even got her name, but I loved the lesson and carry it with me to this day.

Chakra Faerie: Pencil sketch

THE BANSHEE

After my mother died in 2003, I spent a lot of time thinking about death. She wasn't just my adored mother; she was my best friend, and the hole her death left in my world is still cavernous. I try every day to carry forward her heart and her zest, although I still can't seem to accomplish her wit. She was the master and had the best, most disgusting sense of humor EVER!

It was through my grief that I experienced this presence known as the Banshee. The Banshee is found primarily in the British Isles as being the forbearer of death and tragedy. Her terrifying, woeful screams have been heard for centuries, forecasting mortality, trauma and catastrophe to those who are unfortunate enough to hear her. The spirit isn't scary itself, but what she forecasts is.

Banshee: Pencil sketch

JESUS, MOTHER & MARY

Before my Uncle John passed away, he asked me to do a special project for him. He said, of all the images, paintings, and drawings of Jesus he had seen in his lifetime, he had never seen one of Jesus smiling. He wanted me to create a "Smiling Jesus," which further inspired me to draw one of Mother Mary and of Mary Magdalene. I know it's hard to see skin color in a pencil sketch, but none of them were light-complected...

Smiling Jesus: Pencil sketch

Mother Mary: Pencil sketch

Mary Magdalene: Pencil sketch

THE ANGELS

I've always held a certain affinity for the Angels. What great guys they are! I mean, they're androgynous, so they're neither male nor female, but to me, they emit a very masculine energy. I guess you would need balls in a figurative way to do God's bidding.

I've had several encounters with what I considered to be Angels. The most memorable was Samael. I know many religions consider him to be demonic, but I believe he's vastly misunderstood. He's an Angel of death, which explains why there's a negative stigma attached to him. My encounter with him came early one morning as I was trying to get my ass out of bed. I saw a shimmering glow at the foot of my bed, kind of like the transporters on Star Trek. It was so pretty!

I reached out to inquire who this spirit was. He said his name was Samael. It kind of panicked me to hear his name. I know Angels don't usually drop by for a cup of coffee and morning gossip, so I asked why he was there. He responded with "I'm just checking in." I accepted his answer, with reservations, and he faded away.

Later that night, my mother died. Her unexpected passing came as a complete shock to all of us. I know Samael was there to help her cross over and I'm forever grateful to him for that; not everyone is ushered into the afterlife by the Angel of Death himself. Godspeed, Mary Theresa Coffman. 11/10/2003.

This experience deepened my appreciation for Angels, and I immersed myself in their energy. Uriel was one of my favorites and I did several sketches of him. Here's to the joy of Angels and for all they do because they love us.

Uriel, The Flame of God: Ink sketch

Uriel: Pencil sketch

Samael: Pencil sketch

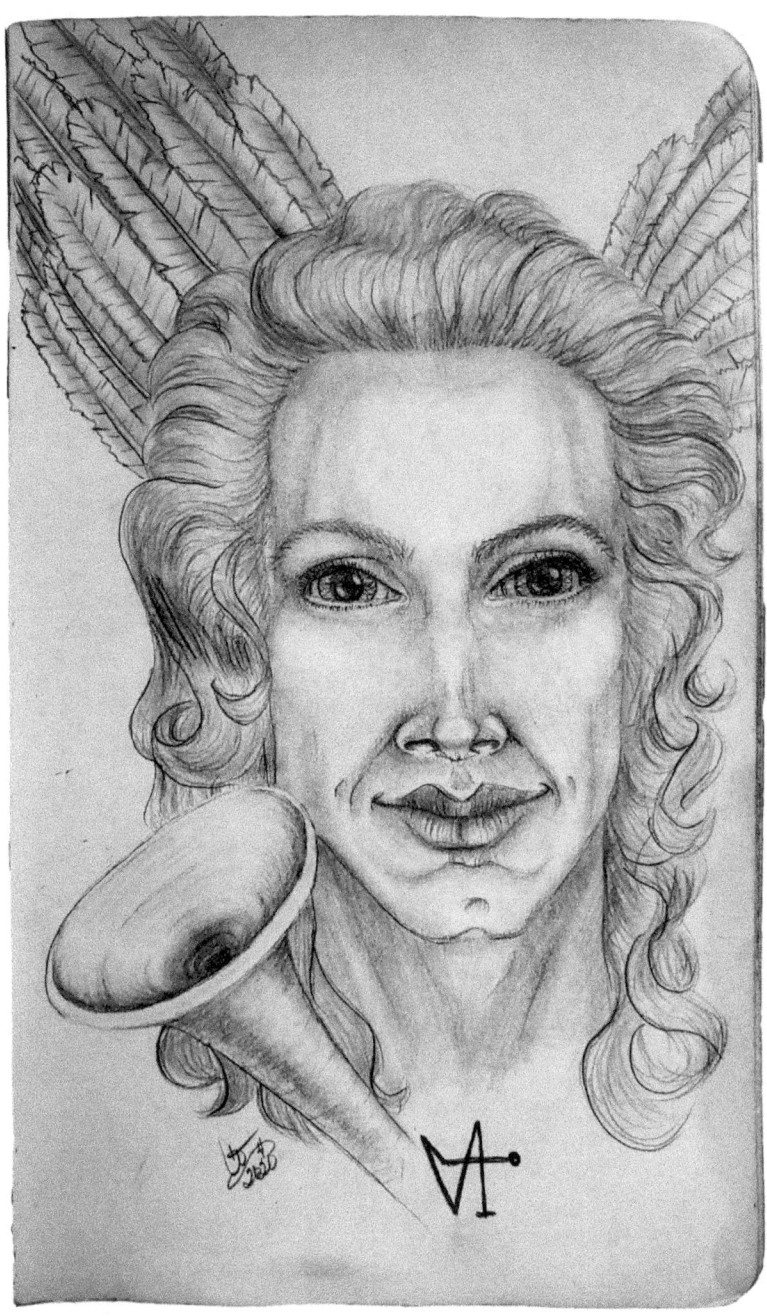

"Raphael" pencil sketch

"Michael" pencil sketch

"Gabriel" pencil sketch

THE BAD BOYS SECTION

In the early part of 2003, an unexpected thing happened. An entity visited in my meditation, who called himself Felonious. He wasn't a friendly-looking dude, and his vibes were dangerous.

I immediately put up my guard and asked him why he was coming to me. He replied, "I want you to draw me in your book." I was a little taken aback by this request, but I agreed with the condition that he would behave himself while he was there and leave as soon as it was complete. He complied. You could certainly feel him being around, but he never stepped a foot out of line and as soon as I finished the drawing, he was gone and I've never seen him again.

After that, I had many entities come to me with the same request. I always gave them the same stipulations and they also conformed. Still, to this day, I have spirits, entities and energies come to me for a portrait. I've only refused one and that's because the bitch wouldn't comply with my rules. Yes, she's a bitch and proud of it, but I refused to give her any more life than she already has. It was obvious to me that her intentions were not the same as the others.

Anyways, here are a number of portraits I was asked to draw. Some of them are familiar and some of them aren't; some are scary and some will give you goosebumps; but all of them know how to mind their manners and stay true to their word.

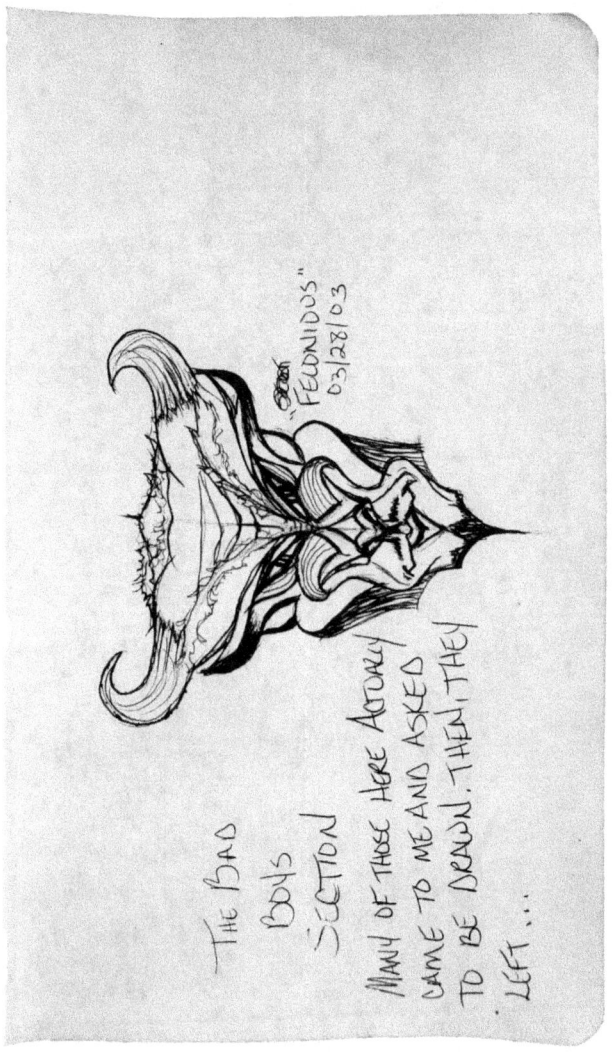

Felonious: Ink sketch with notes

A Furry Guy: Ink sketch

The Succubus: Ink sketch

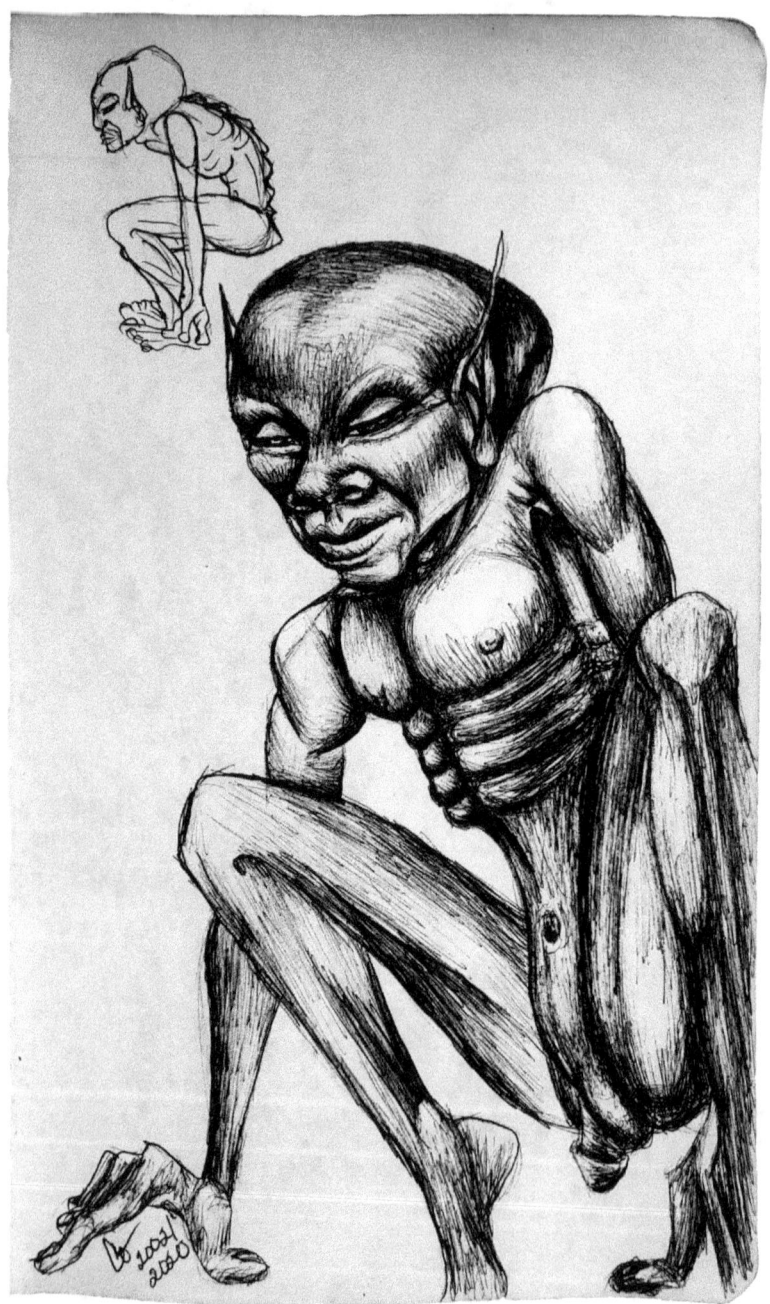

The Basement Dweller: Ink sketch

El Chupacabra: Pencil sketch

PORTRAIT OF A DEMON

This dude needs a bit of explanation. He's another who came to me for a portrait. He made a special point of making sure I included both sets of his hands. Often, an entity will explain certain parts of their anatomy that have either been misinterpreted or ignored in other works of art or in legend. I thought it was cool that he has hands on his wings, as well as hands like we do. How useful!

While I was in the middle of drawing his portrait, my son came to me with a drawing of his own. He was confused and a little frightened that he had been seeing this demon, not to mention he felt compelled to draw it. I almost fell out of my chair when he showed me his drawing. It was identical to mine. I showed him my sketch and told him the story. I kept his drawing with mine for many years, but it was unfortunately lost when my diary went on its great adventure.

The Demon: Pencil sketch

PADRE PIO

Padre Pio, now known as Saint Pio of Pietrelcina, has been in my life since before he was venerated. He was a Capuchin monk born in 1887 and a true stigmatist. His hands started bleeding when he was only 15 years old and were completely healed only after his death.

He first made an appearance in my world with the scent of roses and a comforting vibe when I truly needed some solace. I'm not Catholic, but I certainly appreciate the love this man showed me in some of my darkest hours. He's been coming through for many years and after drawing the demon portrait, I brought in the energy of Padre Pio to help cleanse the residual vibes.

Padre Pio: Pencil sketch

'OLE MAN STULL

Now, here's a crazy story for you. Many years before I started this diary, I was heavily involved with the PRS (Psychical Research Society) as a psychic consultant. I did readings, paranormal investigations, past life regressions and much more. I met and worked with a lot of people during that time.

One night, about 1990, I had a dream that I was in a cemetery with a bunch of college kids. We were checking out an abandoned church on the property when an old man with coal-black eyes popped out of the ground, raging at us, and scaring the snot out of everyone. He chased us with a shovel into the back of a red pickup, which we used to escape. He pursued us all the way to the gate at the road.

That's when my phone rang and woke me up a little after 3 am. On the other end, was a young lady from Lawrence, KS I had done some readings for. She was in a frenzy, terrified and babbling incoherently. Once I got her calmed down enough to understand what she was saying, it became clear my dream and her experience were related. She told me that she and her friends paid a late-night visit to Stull Cemetery but had been chased out by a demonic old man who came out of the ground. I gingerly asked if they were in a red pickup. When she confirmed they were, I choked and sputtered a little.

Before that night, I had never heard of the Stull Cemetery, but you can bet I did my research after that experience. It's rumored to be a portal to Hell with a long list of paranormal events, dating back to the 1800s. The Gateway to Hell is supposed to open two nights a year on Halloween and on the Spring Equinox. There's even a rumor that Pope John Paul rerouted his plane so as not to fly over this cemetery. None of this is confirmed and it should be easy enough to prove or disprove, but the locals have locked the gates to visitors of any kind. Entering the cemetery will land you in jail with a big fine. I've driven by it several times but never stopped. The last time I drove by on my way to work, as if on cue, the radio started playing Sympathy for the Devil by the Rolling Stones. Call me warped, but it made me laugh.

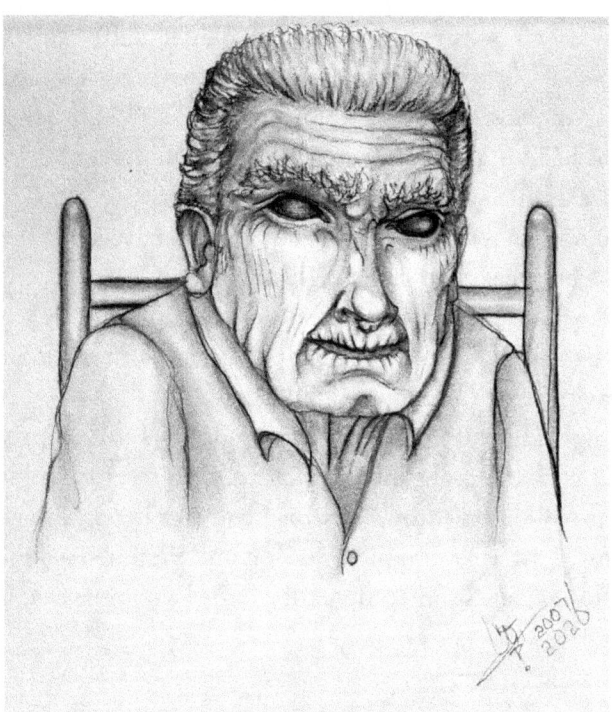

'Ole Man Stull: Pencil sketch

WEREWOLF

How much does reality influence imagination? I've been doing special effects makeup since I was 10 years old. It all started when my dad played Dracula in a Jaycee's haunted house, and it has since evolved into a career of makeup, costuming, and FX on many movies, live events and in the theater.

In truth, many of the monsters I've created have some basis in my reality; I've been seeing them all my life.

When we were still caretakers at the barn, there were a couple of years we helped the local Elks Club put on a haunted hayride in the field. Everyone loved it, including the Faeries.

One night during the haunted hayride, as I was approaching a crest in the field, I saw one of our werewolf actors in silhouette against the full moon throw back his head and howl. The visual was so stunning, I drew several pictures of it and designed a badass mask based on the image. I sometimes still wonder what inspired him to be so real...

"Bark At The Moon" pencil sketch.

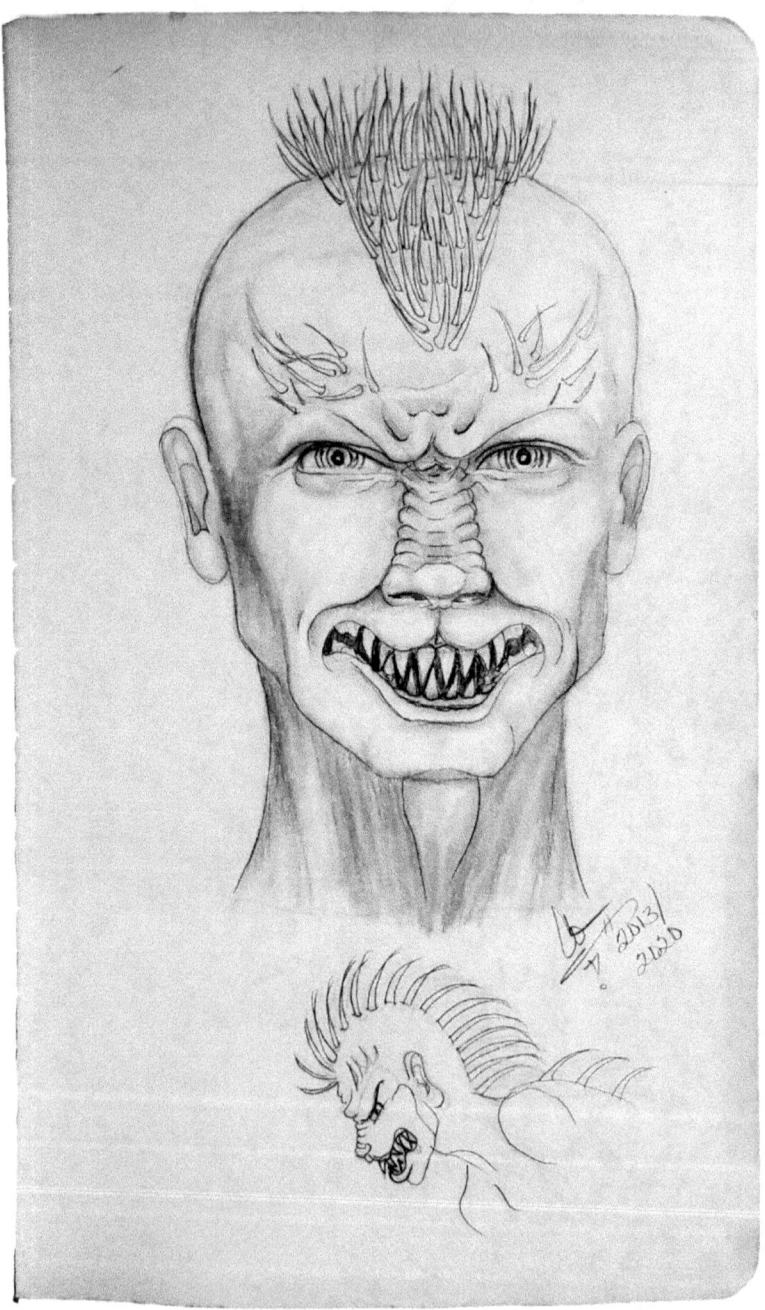

Werewolf Mask: Pencil sketch of design

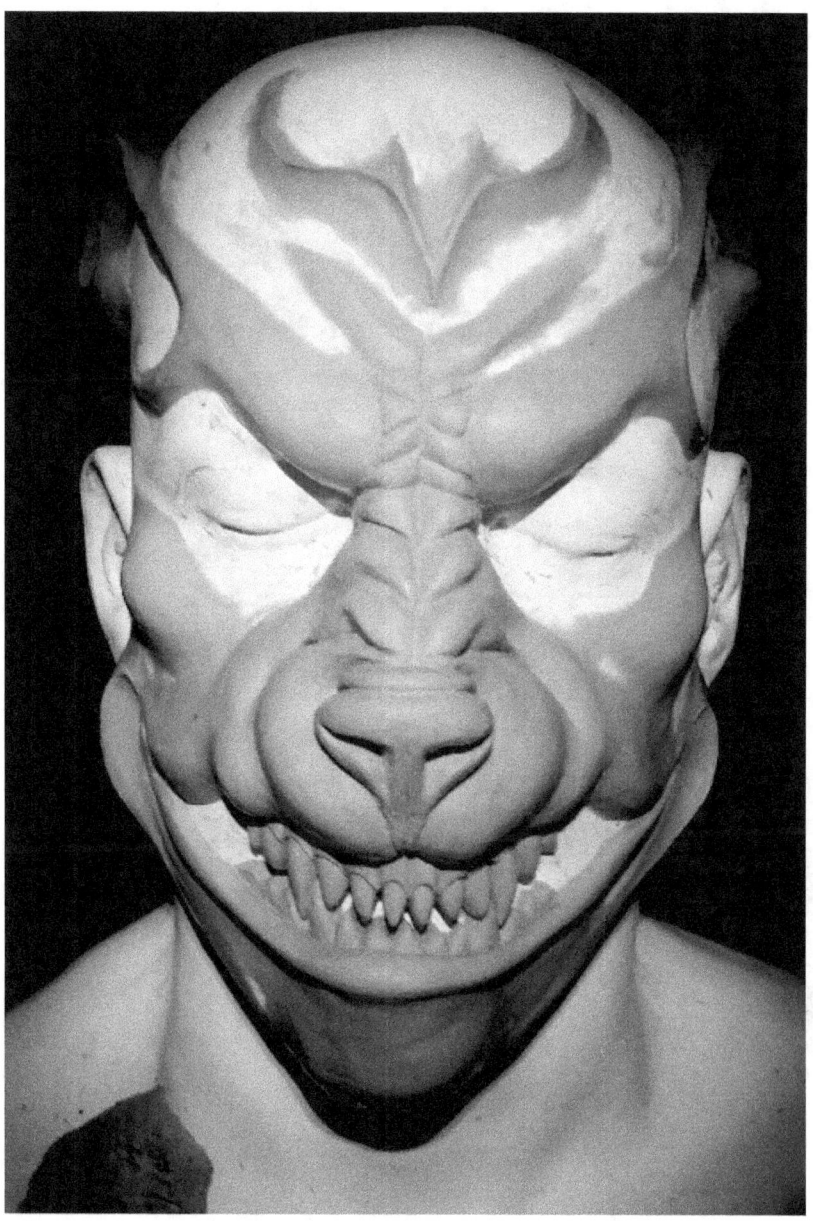

*Werewolf mask clay sculpture on armature. This sculpture was molded. That mold
created the finished mask on the next page.*

Finished Werewolf Mask in silicone with real hair and FX contact lenses. (Photo courtesy of Jordan Bunce)

ABOUT THE AUTHOR

Colleen Coffman has held a lifelong passion for the arts as well as studying all things esoteric–earthly and otherwise. She's spent the last 25 years in film and theater as a special effects artist, winning many awards and garnering more entertaining escapades than you can shake a stick at. She also happens to have an affinity for storytelling and taps a variety of mediums with her incredible talents, so she can share her greatest adventures and ever-evolving vision with the world. A devoted mother, daughter, sister, aunt, grandmother and nurturer of her great extended family, she thrives on taking people along on her colorful and exciting journey through life, and we're all better for it!

AFTERWORD

Go to <u>hangarıpublishing.com</u> to learn more about the Authors and stay up to date with their newest releases.

www.ingramcontent.com/pod-product-compliance
Lightning Source LLC
Chambersburg PA
CBHW071207120626
46546CB00006B/2453